Ransom Neutron Stars
Steel Pan Traffic Jam
by Cath Jones
Illustrated by Sonny Ross

Published by Ransom Publishing Ltd.
Unit 7, Brocklands Farm, West Meon, Hampshire GU32 1JN, UK
www.ransom.co.uk

ISBN   978 178591 430 0
First published in 2017

Steel Pan
Traffic Jam

Cath Jones

Illustrated by Sonny Ross

Ransom

Tam sits on the top step with her twin, Bartt.

She sips a cup of coffee and asks her brother, "What shall we do?"

Fixing things is hard. Now they need some fun!

"Can you hear that?" asks Tam.

She thinks she can hear a band.

Bartt is not sure.

They run down the street.

"Look!" yells Tam. "It is a steel pan band."

Just then, **CRASH! BANG! BOING!**

It is coming from a big red van.

A window is down.

Tam peeps in.

"How fantastic! The van is full of steel

pan drums."

A man gets out. This is Mick.

Mick spent a lot of cash on steel pans.

Now he has all this gear

for a steel pan band.

"Can we join in?" asks Tam.

Mick looks at Tam.

"Let's see!"

He gets Tam to clap her hands.

Can she do it? Bartt is sure she can.

Yes! Tam claps her hands just right.
Good. Now Tam can get a steel pan.

Tam stands next to Mick. The steel pan
hangs from a strap on her neck.
She keeps a good grip on the stick.

Mick taps a spot on the drum.

Tam hits the spot.

Then Mick points at lots of stickers on the steel pan. Tam hits them all.

Tam hits her drum hard.

Mick grins.

"No need to hit it so hard, Tam!"

Bartt gets a steel pan next.

He hits it just as hard as his sister!

Mick grins again.

"Not bad!"

Mick asks Bartt and Tam, "Have you ever been on a festival float?"

No, they have not.

"OK, come with me."

Mick's steel pan band is in this festival!

Tam and Bartt will be on a festival float right now.

Are they afraid? No.

(Well, OK, a little bit!)

Tam can smell food. It must be supper.

"The steel pan band must have some food," Mick tells them. "This is my gran's chicken."

Is it roast chicken?

No, it is Jamaican jerk chicken.

Mick's gran is a good cook and she has got jerk chicken for the band! Yum!

Wow! Look at that festival with lots of
floats and flags.

Now all the steel pans are on the float.
Bartt and Tam get onto the float and
wait.

Mick gets a banner from the van.
It has a black, green and yellow flag
on it. It is the Jamaican flag.

The banner is for the float.
Tam thinks the float looks smart.

Then Mick frowns and groans.

"What now?" Tam asks Mick.

"The float needs to go down the street, but it will not go. It will not start."

All the other floats are stuck too.

They cannot turn back.

They have to wait.

It is a steel pan traffic jam!

Mick rings the Green Flag breakdown truck, but they cannot fix the van now.

Tam and Bartt jump down from the float. Tam can fix it! It is her job to fix stuff.

Tam grabs a spanner and creeps under the van.

It is an oil drip. No problem!

Mick is so glad!

Now the festival floats can go down the street.

Tam can see a big crowd.

Mick has a big tub on the float. When Tam looks in it, she sees it is full of coins from the crowd.

Tam is glad. The coins will help the steel pan band.

At the end, Tam helps Mick put the steel pans back in the van.

Will she see him next week?

Yes!

She and Bartt will get better
and better on the steel pans.

Ransom Neutron Stars

Steel Pan Traffic Jam
Word count **594**

Covers:
Letters and Sounds Phase 4

Phonics

Phonics 1 Not Pop, Not Rock
Go to the Laptop Man
Gus and the Tin of Ham

Phonics 2 Deep in the Dark Woods
Night Combat
Ben's Jerk Chicken Van

Phonics 3 GBH
Steel Pan Traffic Jam
Platform 7

Phonics 4 The Rock Show
Gaps in the Brain
New Kinds of Energy

Book bands

Pink Curry!
Free Runners
My Toys

Red Shopping with Zombies
Into the Scanner
Planting My Garden

Yellow Fit for Love
The Lottery Ticket
In the Stars

Blue Awesome ATAs
Wolves
The Giant Jigsaw

Green Fly, May FLY!
How to Start Your Own
Crazy Cult
The Care Home

Orange Text Me
The Last Soldier
Best Friends

Before reading

Look at the book cover
Ask, "What do you think

To build independence,
at the start of this book.

back to pages 6 and 7 in 4a and read the words again with
the child.

During reading

Offer plenty of support and praise as the child reads the story.
Listen carefully and respond to events in the text.

In 4c, the new **Key Words** are not shown at the bottom of
the page. If the child hesitates over a word, turn to the back
of the book to practise reading it together. If the word is
phonically decodable, you can sound out the letters and
blend the sounds to read the word ("d-o-g, dog"). Praise the
child for their effort, then return to the story.

Pause every few pages and ask questions to check the child's
understanding of what they have read. If they begin to lose
concentration, stop reading and save the page for later.

Celebrate the child's achievement and come back to the
story the next day.

After reading

After reading this book, ask, "Did you enjoy the story? What did
you like about it?" Encourage the child to share their opinions.

Use the comprehension questions on page 54 to check the
child's understanding and recall of the text.

Ladybird

Series Consultant: Professor David Waugh
With thanks to Kulwinder Maude

LADYBIRD BOOKS

UK | USA | Canada | Ireland | Australia
India | New Zealand | South Africa

Ladybird Books is part of the Penguin Random House group of companies
whose addresses can be found at global.penguinrandomhouse.com.
www.penguin.co.uk   www.puffin.co.uk   www.ladybird.co.uk

 Penguin
Random House
UK

Original edition of Key Words with Peter and Jane first published by Ladybird Books Ltd 1964
Series updated 2023
This book first published 2023
001

Text copyright © Ladybird Books Ltd, 1964, 2023
Illustrations by Gustavo Mazali
Illustrations copyright © Ladybird Books Ltd, 2023

With thanks to Liz Pemberton for her contributions in advising on the illustrations
With thanks to Inclusive Minds for connecting us with their Inclusion Ambassador network,
and in particular thanks to Guntaas Kaur Chugh for her input on the illustrations

Printed in China

The authorized representative in the EEA is Penguin Random House Ireland,
Morrison Chambers, 32 Nassau Street, Dublin D02 YH68

A CIP catalogue record for this book is available from the British Library

ISBN: 978-0-241-51084-1

All correspondence to:
Ladybird Books
Penguin Random House Children's
One Embassy Gardens, 8 Viaduct Gardens, London SW11 7BW

Key Words

with Peter and Jane

4c

School friends

Based on the original
Key Words with Peter and Jane
reading scheme and research by William Murray

Original edition written by William Murray
This edition written by Shari Last
Illustrated by Gustavo Mazali

Peter and Jane are
at school.

It is "Play with Friends"
week at Peter and
Jane's school.

"Have fun playing with
friends!" says Mum.

RED TRE

7

The children have some good friends at school.

"We can have good fun this week, Will!" says Jane.

Peter sees bears, boats and trains at school.

"I like that bear," says Amber.

"And me," says Peter.

Peter and Amber sit down with a boy and a girl.

The friends see some boats.

"One red boat," says Peter.

13

The children see a red train station.

"A red train station. I like train stations," says Peter.

"'Play with Friends' week is good fun! I like playing with the train station and the boats," says Amber.

Here are Jane and Will.

"Look, a red train!"
says Jane.

"Can you help me with
a train?" says Will.

Jane likes helping
friends.

"It is a school. The girl is helping the boy at the school," says Pippa.

"That is a good school!" says Jane.

21

The boys and girls
want to give some hay
to the school rabbits.

One rabbit hops up to Jane.

"I see some rabbit friends! Come down and have some hay," says Jane.

"That was good," says Will.

"It was fun to give hay to the rabbits," says Jane.

The children sit down for tea at school.

"Tea! Tea! I can see some red fruit," says Peter.

The boys and girls have the red fruit.

"Some fruit for you and some fruit for me," says Jane.

"Can the bear have some fruit?" says Peter.

"Here is a red one," says Amber.

Peter gives the bear one red fruit.

"We can give the dog some fruit for tea," says Amber.

"Yes!" says Peter.

The dog has some fruit.

The children are playing.

Some boys and girls go up and up and up.

"Look at me up here!" says Jane.

Some children go down and down and down.

"Going down that red one was good fun," says Amber.

39

The children go into school.

"See you, Peter," says Jane.

41

"Look at me! I see a boat for me," says Amber.

"Please help me, Amber. Help me pick one hat!" says Peter.

"The bear wants a bed," says Amber.

The children give the bear a bed.

"The bear's bed is red like Jane's," says Peter.

45

Here is the train station.

Peter helps one train get down to the station.

"This is a good train!" says Amber.

47

"I want this boat to have a red sail," says Jane.

"I can give you some help with the boat. Friends help friends," says Will.

49

"That is a good bed!
I can see some legs for
the bed. Here are some
red ones," says Jane.

School was good fun.

"See you!" say the children's friends.

Questions

Answer these questions about the story.

1 What toys does Peter see first at school?

2 What do Jane and Will give to the rabbits?

3 What do Peter and Amber give the bear and the dog for tea?

4 Will says, "Friends help friends." How does he help Jane?